FICTIONS

FICTIONS

ELAND MANN

CONVERSATION PUBLISHING

Printed in the United States of America.
First paperback edition October 2021.

10 9 8 7 6 5 4 3 2 1

Cover and layout design by G Sharp Design, LLC.
www.gsharpmajor.com

ISBN 978-1-7359415-8-5 (paperback)
ISBN 978-1-7359415-9-2 (ebook)

Published by Conversation Publishing.
www.conversationpublishing.com

To X. I *found my treasure when* I *found you.*

Contents

A Word from the Author

"I am not sure that I exist, actually. I am all the writers that I have read, all the people that I have met, all the women that I have loved, all the cities I have visited."
Jorge Luis Borges

"Once gone through, we trace the round again; and are infants, boys, and men, and Ifs eternally."
Herman Melville, *Moby-Dick*

"Of all the inanimate objects, of all men's creations, books are the nearest to us for they contain our very thoughts, our ambitions, our indignations, our illusions, our fidelity to the truth, and our persistent leanings to error. But most of all they resemble us in their precious hold on life."
Joseph Conrad

THE OLDEST OF these stories, "The Gondolier," I wrote in the fall of 2012 while living in Los Angeles, CA. For years I had wanted to write a story about a lovesick Venetian gondolier, perhaps setting it during World War II where it could function as a war story *and* a love story. I knew little (nothing) about Italy, Ethiopia, war, or the life of a gondolier when I started typing. But I wrote the story with confidence, nonetheless, because I felt I finally knew a little something about love.

I completed "The Gondolier" over the course of two or three weekends. I immediately followed it with "The Surgeon" and "Trap Street, USA," both of which dealt not with love but with doubt, self-pity, and failed expectations—three other things I felt I knew something about.

While living in Ulaanbaatar, Mongolia, it was my privilege to belong to the "Wayword Scribblers," a creative writing group of five or six ex-pat journalists and would-be writers. We'd meet for drinks, swap stories, and do writing exercises. The audience (and accountability) helped me complete "Shaco's Death," "The Year of the Marmot," and "Somalis?" in 2015.

I wrote "The 10-Million-Dollar Pillow" while living in Charleston, SC. I started the story in 2016, in the midst of grieving the death of Javha, my brother-in-law. I returned to the story in 2017 or 2018, when I was finally back in a state of mind that allowed me to finish something I'd started.

In 2021, while preparing to publish this volume, I conceived of and wrote "The Delivery." By the time of its writing, I had become a father to two toddlers and felt I knew a little about modern parenthood.

Several of these stories are set in locales I haven't visited: the Peruvian Amazon; early 20th-century Ethiopia; the Indian Ocean off Somalia; Varanasi, India. It's my hope that these settings lend more enjoyment, perspective, and meaning to the story than had I set them entirely within the realm of my firsthand experience.

It's been a decade-long journey to complete these stories and publish this book. While I don't have much to say about my life over this decade aside from what's written in these fictions, I do have a lot of gratitude.

Thank you to Keith Farrell, my friend and business partner, who helped me turn my love of writing into a profession I'm proud of. Thank you to the hundreds of authors I've worked with who shared with me their passion for creating something great. Thank you to Khaliuna Mann, my wife and best friend, who helped me chase my dreams. And thank you to Marlowe and Lincoln, my children, who I love with all my heart.

Eland Mann, August 2021

The Year of
the Marmot

OR SEVERAL YEARS running a few acquaintances and I held a small gathering at my apartment to celebrate in an offhand way the Chinese New Year. None of us were Chinese, nor was there an Orientalist among us, but we always found ourselves looking for relief from the dreary mid-winter cold, and enjoyed the red glow of Chinese lanterns and the warmth of plum wine.

This past February we rang in the Year of the Snake with particular enthusiasm. This was partly because I had come into some money and had moved into a new apartment better suited to more extravagant get-togethers. It was also partly because a dear friend of mine brought along the woman he was enamored with at the time, Wu Lin, an in-the-flesh Chinese firecracker.

The highlight of the evening was a horoscope reading performed by Wu Lin, who had brought along a book on the Chinese Zodiac, and who proceeded to read to each delighted guest, one by one, their fortune for the coming year. The readings amused us, as our fortunes often contained odd details that seemed more in line with the life of a rural Chinese peasant. When it was my turn, Wu Lin revealed I was to have an exceptional year, as long as I refrained from one activity—I was forbidden from eating marmot meat.

> The readings amused us, as our fortunes often contained odd details that seemed more in line with the life of a rural Chinese peasant.

I'd never heard of a marmot, let alone considered eating its meat. The ban shouldn't have mattered. You'd never guess that this innocuous moment was the beginning of my condition.

The following day, a light hangover dulled my appetite. I nibbled on some flavorless leftovers but nothing more, and went to bed early.

The next afternoon I met several friends at a new bistro that had opened in my neighborhood. I was still not feeling hungry, but ordered a sandwich anyway and forced half of it down. My friends remarked at the excellent taste of the food. My sandwich was cardboard bland, but I was beginning to feel unwell, and mentioned nothing.

Over the next week I attempted to eat twenty different meals. I ate favorite dishes of mine at home, at restaurants, and at a friend's house. With each passing meal, it became more painfully clear that I had lost my sense of taste. I would hover over the food before eating, smelling nothing. Before each bite, I would pray for any flavor that could satisfy. And at night, awake in bed, I'd close my eyes and imagine a decadent buffet of filet mignon and steamed mussels, lamb chops and grilled sea bass, moist pastries and elegant chocolate desserts, each dish more delicious than the last. Yet the only food, real or imagined, that could make my mouth water, that could get my gut grumbling and have me licking my lips in ecstasy, was the thought of marmot meat.

By March I had lost twenty pounds. I bought a new belt. Friends and colleagues became so worried that I saw a doctor at their insistence, but after weeks of tests he determined my condition to have no physical origin.

"If a dead tongue is the only symptom, then the likely cause is psychological," said the doctor, pressing a pamphlet into my hands and referring me to a psychiatrist.

When a cold hunger takes hold in the depths of your stomach, you begin to fathom ideas never before considered. (Ideas like gutting a live, squealing marmot, stripping its coarse fur, tearing its bloody raw meat with your teeth, gnawing the last of its cartilage off the bones, cutting your tongue on its jagged bones as you hollow out the marrow, feeling satisfied at long last as the fatty flesh fills your stomach.)

Your being roars, as your lack of taste carves you into an empty cavern, engorged with the echoes of your growling stomach. You long to fill the void with marmot meat. You are gradually consumed by the idea of consuming.

The most terrible part of your condition is that you have no idea how to get any marmot meat.

Shaco's Death

Diego C—, Spanish Geographical Society, Peru

IT WAS A complete shock. I couldn't believe the words, spoken through the sat-phone by my grad student embedded deep in the Peruvian Amazon. "Shaco's dead."

Shaco the aged Matsigenka guide, who knew each bend of the serpentine Madre de Dios River better than any man alive. Shaco the gray-haired gardener, who tended a plot on a sun-soaked river island near the peaceful frontier village of Diamante. Shaco the gregarious friend, who was the only local to communicate with Peru's most recluse tribe, the Mascho-Piro. Shaco the six days dead, a Mascho-Piro arrow through his heart.

I heard the news of Shaco's death and immediately took a boat upriver to Diamante. There I visited his wife and family, who had retreated to the village out of fear after the arrow, propelled from the bush by a member of the isolated Mascho-Piro, had punctured Shaco's heart.

Diamante men had recovered Shaco's body the following day, and after a well-attended ceremony they buried him in the manner of the locals.

I had trouble understanding the reason behind Shaco's death.

He, the two grad students on my geographic expedition, and I had been the last outsiders to see the Mascho-Piro, one of the few remaining recluse tribes of the Peruvian Amazon. They hadn't been photographed for thirty years, until several months ago during the dry season when I snapped a group of young Mascho-Piro men with painted faces and loin clothes standing about the east bank of the calm Madre de Dios.

A stout member of the Mascho-Piro had hailed our motorboat then as I clicked away with my camera.

What does he say? asked one grad student.

"Go away, idiots," said the other.

No, replied Shaco. He is asking for machetes.

We watched them closely as we passed and rounded a bend.

> *In speaking with the locals of Diamante, it was their opinion that Shaco wasn't a bridge.*

In speaking with the locals of Diamante, it was their opinion that Shaco wasn't a bridge. He was just a local native, assimilated, who happened to marry a Piro woman and understand a bit of the Mascho-Piro language. He was a farmer on a mid-river island, only speaking or trading with the Mascho-Piro once a year or so. He wasn't a missionary or an agent of progress, pushing the frontier jungle. He wasn't an arrow propelled across the river into the heart of the Mascho-Piro.

Together the villagers and I mourned his loss over cups of masato, and wondered in silence about those unknowns that lurk in the bush, that eye one another from opposite banks. What chasm between them had made Shaco their casualty?

I had a talk to give at the Spanish Geographical Society in Lima the next week, so I was scheduled to depart Diamante the following morning on a boat heading downriver. Before I left the village, I made a visit to Shaco's abandoned island. I wasn't worried about a repeat attack, as the locals said there had been no reported sightings of the Mascho-Piro since Shaco's death.

As the early morning sun rose above the tree line, I stood in the garden patch, weeds already beginning to sprout in the half-tilled ground. I looked across the island and the river into the dense foliage on the far eastern banks, retracing the arc of the fatal arrow with my eyes. In that moment I glimpsed what Shaco saw in the moments before his death, after collapsing in his garden patch, yards from a river eddy that swirled against the current. The eddy's upstream motion gave that patch of river an emerald tint, an anomalous sight in the otherwise muddy Madre de Dios. Such a hue would be remarkable, were it not for the surging, looping, ever-thickening mass of green closing in around us on all sides.

I could almost feel the arrow pierce my heart. And then I left that place.

The Surgeon

AFTER 2,029 OPEN-HEART procedures, 58 deaths during convalescence, 117 failures under the knife, sixteen congenital, unavoidable demises, sixty-three articles in the *Journal of Medicine* (a dozen or so the standards in their field), two failed marriages, two failed relationships with otherwise successful children, and one lauded stint as Chief of Surgery at the thirteenth ranked hospital for Cardiology and Cardiac Surgery in the United States, Dr. Raskhan Shukla—balding, but without the paunch he remembered budding from the midsection of his father, due to his weekend hikes in the mountains around the city and his weeks where he spent an average of fifty-seven hours on his feet at work—renowned heart surgeon, had found himself alone in his Mercedes on his way to an empty home, when the freeway's pattern of white headlights and red taillights recalled to him the vague ornamentation of some forgotten shrine, its flickering votives and spiced scents, and he realized he was still alive.

He told his colleagues he was leaving to spend the remainder of his days fly-fishing clear mountain streams, and watched their eyes dim as they wished him luck, and told him to enjoy himself. Only the woman at the American Airlines ticket counter and the TSA agent who glanced at his boarding pass knew of his one-way ticket to Varanasi, on the banks of the Ganges, with layovers in Shanghai and Delhi. The trip, the first return to his native country in 51 years, took 33 hours. He savored the taste of the dirty martini on his tongue as he left the air-conditioned safety of the plane, for he knew, as a blast of heat and the echo of Hindi surged down the jetway, that this was the last trace of habitual comfort he was to experience before the chaos of India overwhelmed him.

He spent several idle days acclimating to his new environment from the balcony of his modest hotel, taking the city's pulse, until his feet grew restless. At the end of his first week, he found himself descending the steps of the Manikarnika Ghat, one of the many stairwells around the city leading directly into the Ganges, when he stopped to observe the unusual number of fires burning on the banks and barges about the crowded river.

"Manikarnika Ghat is always burning," remarked a cross-legged yogi seated on the stone steps. "Many come to Varanasi to die. To die here is to end the cycle of death and reincarnation."

The heart surgeon turned to the yogi. "Is that why you are here?"

"Yes," said the yogi, "and no."

The surgeon noticed thick layers of soot darkened the facades of every building in the vicinity.

"There was a temple I once visited as a child," said the surgeon. "I wonder if you might know its location. I think it must not be far from here. There was always a great quantity of sandalwood incense in the air about the temple, but it never entirely masked the smell of smoke lingering from the cremations nearby. The temple was for Krishna, and portrayed him standing on a large serpent."

"Such a temple I know well," said the yogi. "I will guide you."

The temple with the sandalwood incense and the trodden serpent was as the surgeon remembered.

Over the next several months, the surgeon spent an average of 57 hours a week on his knees at the temple, in prayer and meditation. On weekends he stretched his legs by wandering the city, with the occasional pause to rub away a cramp. After several months, despite his devoted prostration, thoughts of his Mercedes on the freeway, primetime television, and steak (for the love of Brahma, steak!) still clouded his meditation. Even worse, there were times late at night when, on the verge of sleep, his deepest memories would gash a hole into his heart and leak into his being. He would stare at the wooden beams of his hotel room ceiling, eyeing coiled, dark knots of failed techniques and flat-lines; of youthful first kisses and childhood friends; of tempered dreams. In those moments he was helpless, his breath cut short, tears in his eyes. He would fall asleep only after the regret—pulsing through his body as thick as poisoned blood—had subsided. He always expected to wake up with a bruised chest.

He would fall asleep only after the regret—pulsing through his body as thick as poisoned blood—had subsided.

Early one morning, after one such night, he found himself unable to return to sleep, and sought the sanctuary of the temple. As he knelt before Krishna, he noticed the presence of two seated yogis beneath an awning on the other side of the temple courtyard. By their ochre-stained robes and chalked faces, he knew them to be wandering sadhus, the most sacred and devoted of yogis. One sat in meditation with his eyes closed and right arm extended above his head. The other seemed to await the surgeon's presence, his eyes open. The surgeon pressed his palms together and approached the sadhus.

"Babaji," the surgeon implored, to the sadhu with the open eyes. "Do you feel pain?"

The sadhu sat motionless. The surgeon was unsure whether he had been heard.

"Babaji," the surgeon began again, but he stopped when the sadhu with the raised arm opened his eyes.

"That one does not speak," said the raised-arm sadhu, nodding to his silent companion. "He has taken a vow of silence, to show his devotion to Krishna."

"You have not taken the vow?"

"I have," said the sadhu, "but I have renounced my right arm. I have kept it raised, for twelve years."

"And do you feel pain?"

"No longer," the sadhu replied. "But for years the pain was excruciating. My arm is now dead."

The surgeon stared at the emaciated limb, its every joint and muscle long atrophied. The sadhu's fingers appeared fused together in a crumpled knot. Shoots of twisted yellow fingernails dangled far below his wrist.

"Babaji," the surgeon said after a pause. "I want to exist above my memories and separate myself from my feelings. Might I take a vow to renounce my heart?"

The other sadhu, silent and open-eyed, gestured for the surgeon to sit down.

Over the next several years, as the surgeon wandered from village to village— his days and nights occupied with fasts and meditations, his newly ascetic life led without possessions—he became increasingly less troubled by the memories that had once prevented his sleep. On the occasional, blissful night when his mind not once succumbed to recollection, he slept as if a man reborn.

And with every conscious moment he renounced his heart.

His progress continued until one night, seated upright and drifting comfortably off to sleep, he felt a violent, uncontrollable spasm in his torso. He suppressed the pain and staggered from his lodgings at a village temple, finally collapsing beside a country road.

He awoke wrapped in white sheets, in a soft bed, an invasion of formaldehyde and bleach in his nose. It was his first return to a hospital in nearly a decade; but he was not immediately conscious of this, for the pain in his chest had not yet subsided. His heart pulsed in agony, each pang reversing an entire year of austere devotion. The pangs intensified until he buckled upright and was sick. During the half-second of pain-trumping nausea, he realized what he needed to do. He jumped from the bed and hurriedly stumbled about in the darkness of the slumbering hospital, collecting the requisite supplies before returning to bed.

He acknowledged a noiseless scream from some dormant recess within his mind as he made the first incision, ignored it as he slid the scalpel along the flesh, down the middle of his chest. He daubed away the blood with a cloth to clean the white sternum beneath. When his fingers scraped dry bone, his hand leapt for the oscillating saw, as if a day had not passed since his last surgery. Decades of experience enabled him to breach his chest in less than 30 seconds; yet nothing but spiritual devotion prepared him for the discomfort of dismantling his own ribcage. The two halves of his chest he forced apart with a clamp-like chest spreader, exposing the wet inner cavity amidst a mild spray of torn blood vessels and a slurp of shifting suction. As the surgeon notched the instrument toward its final position, he congratulated himself on his fortitude to stay conscious. There was but one last step. With his chin pressed against his collarbone and scalpel in hand, the surgeon reached into his chest to extricate the one muscle that had tortured him his entire life.

But it was as he had always feared. It took him only a second to understand the truth. After years of medical school lectures, textbook diagrams, and lab dissections; after decades of experience and thousands of hours spent observing, cutting, and repairing the pulsating red organ, Dr. Raskhan Shukla, expert surgeon, discovered something new. He discovered he was different. No spongy tissue throbbed between his lungs. No muscle pumped blood to the rest of his body. Between the aorta and the inferior vena cava was empty space. He strained his eyes and saw only a black void within his chest; nothing to remove, nothing on which to operate. There was no heart to be found. He rested his head against the starched pillow and closed his eyes. After 2,030 procedures, the surgeon's last thought was of reincarnation, for maybe then things might be different.

Somalis?

THE ELDERLY COUPLE would've never referred to themselves as the elderly couple. Retirees, yes, but not elderly. Jim was pals with everybody onboard, from the crew at the Captain's table to the natives hawking souvenirs to the kids attempting the perfect cannonball on the topside pool. You knew he went to Princeton, rowed crew—his daughter, who's there at school now, in fact, a Junior, on the crew team, just like her old man, how about that?—and was onboard to see a bit of the world, all within two minutes of encountering the tall, trim, wispy-haired man and shaking his hand.

Mrs. Jim, never more than a few steps away, was more elderly in her appearance, and her hearing had gone bad in recent years, but somehow she managed to keep up with her husband, whether on the back of his rented-by-the-hour jet ski, at his heel wading through the crowded market stalls of Zanzibar, or by his side, raising a pair of binoculars (from a matching set of "his and hers" they'd bought before last year's trip to Alaska) to her eyes to scrutinize more closely a strange, skiff-looking motorboat that seemed to be heading toward their cruise ship from the southwest, a damned unusual sight wouldn't you say, dear?

What's that?

I said that motor skiff. There's no land in sight. Where d'you think they come from?

Where do who come from, dear? The skiff? Isn't it from another cruise? The *Victoria* that was in port with us in Zanzibar?

The Victoria that was in port with us in Zanzibar?

That's not a damned pleasure craft, dear. Anybody can see that.

Oh, I see. You're right.

And just look at all those natives? How many do you think they got crammed in there? They can't be headed toward us.

A nearby walkie-talkie—in the hands of a crew-member (whom Jim recognized) patrolling the forward deck—fizzled a message that was unintelligible to Jim and Mrs. Jim. But the fizzle had the effect of startling the native crew-member out a half-cooked daze, or so observed Jim.

Sam, was it? Or Steve? What's the trouble on the walkie? You see the skiff out there headed toward us?

The native crew-member named Sam, or Steve, who heretofore had pleasantly nodded at Jim's many winks and smiles, and who always seemed cool despite the stiff collar of his white sailor's uniform, blinked a fearful look at Mr. and Mrs. Jim, and stated in his best and most careful English, before he darted off, a sentence that would puzzle the retirees for the next several minutes.

What's he say? They play the violins at sunrise?

Something about the sunrise, dear, although that's not until Oh-600.

Well, maybe he meant the sunset, and the violins?

I didn't hear anything about any damned violins, dear.

Jim looked from the empty space where the native crewman had been, then back to the approaching skiff, close enough now to see that they could in fact cram ten natives into the skiff, with enough room for a half-dozen AK-47s and several more machetes.

Or maybe he said Somalis? Jim wondered aloud.

So—what?

Trap Street, USA

PROFESSOR R—— SET down the dribbling faux-antique fountain pen, a gift from the English Department for twenty-five years of dedication, and glared at his brief manuscript (the last words he'd ever compose) with the absorbed eyes of a satisfied madman.

The idleness of others tests me. Good, he thinks. He ponders over inserting a quote by Camus before he settles on simplistic brevity and continues. *I observe in my students a gluttonous participation in matters of Gratification and Entertainment, brought about by an excess of Time and an absence of Discipline.* Whereas I lack in the former but not the latter, he murmurs. His heart accelerates as anger replaces blood. *The occasional student, who excels or strives above the rest, does so only to worship at the altar of straight As. I am a functionless votive in the eyes of my students, flickering, fleeting, existing only to bathe them with my own, wan light. Bright as I've tried to burn, my flame is extinguished now in a puddle of my own heated wax.* Rereading, he likes less the extended metaphor. *But my function is well-defined. I burn, and my light will be seen.* He finds he is no Baudelaire, but it will have to do.

If anyone else (a doting student perhaps) had been present in the home office of Professor R—, or in any other room of his modest suburban house, they would have raised their hand and questioned the wetness of the carpet and the strong, alarming smell of gasoline saturating the air. The Professor, however, was busy. *My fire will burn outside the realm of civilization,* he writes. *My road has led me to freedom.*

When he is finished, he stacks the manuscript in order. He slides it into a large manila envelope. He opens his front door. He walks down his driveway to his mailbox. He inserts the manila envelope into his mailbox. He walks up his driveway to his front door. He takes off his faded pair of shearling slippers. He picks up a heavy plastic gas can. He pours the contents of the gas can over his head. He walks toward the coffee table in his living-room. He picks up a matchbook.

He ignores the unlit candle on the coffee table. He immolates his person. He turns to burning flesh and ash. He continues to exist, through a manuscript in a manila envelope in his mailbox.

In said manuscript, Professor R— writes:

Alone here, at the end of my story—or, more accurately, at the end of my road—it is clear my awareness of the 'Problem' began simply with the death of a postman.

At the end of the twenty-fifth year of my daily routine, the quick glance inside a rusty, creaking mailbox had long since lost its place of importance in my consciousness. I expected nothing worthwhile, received nothing worthwhile, and left it at that. But over the course of several recent weeks, the barren echo of many successive, fruitless creaks finally registered in my brain, and I developed a mild concern. Surely one bill, one annoying flier, one letter would have arrived during that time. But the mailbox stubbornly remained empty.

Around that time a colleague of mine made a remark at work about a departmental notice which had appeared in our monthly newsletter. I was mildly surprised, having neither read the article nor received the newsletter. I related this to my colleague, who told me not to worry, because he'd just forward it to me. I remarked I'd rather avoid reading it by email and wait for a real copy. It was then I learned that the newsletter had gone paperless, as it's better for the environment, and from now on the only way to receive the newsletter was by email. I expressed my regret to my colleague and soon forgot the matter. It was this newly learned fact that dulled my suspicions regarding my postal mail for another week.

There was the creaking; there was the hollow echo. Again and again until, finally, the strangeness of my empty mailbox got the better of me and I called the county number for the Post Office. I asked after J——, who delivered the mail in my ZIP code. They said J—— had recently passed away. I was saddened at the news. I asked when they were going to find a replacement. They informed me a replacement had been found weeks ago, immediately after J——'s death. I expressed dismay, for I had not received any mail in nearly a month. They asked for my name and address, which I relayed to them. They expressed regret. My address did not appear to be in their system. Again I mentioned my ZIP code. Again they expressed regret, but they told me it was strange, and it might take some time but they'll look into it. I contented myself that another found my 'Problem' strange and thanked them.

(How was it that I did not learn of the death of my postman for so long? Once upon a time, I was a daily reader of my local obituaries. But the afternoon paper I had subscribed to for years, a paper which had only recently celebrated its 100th anniversary, had closed its doors a year ago. Today not even a fat, tri-colored Sunday issue plops to rest her bulging coupons on my driveway.)

I did not worry about the death of the postman, nor contemplated again the interruption of my mail, until the following week, when I discovered the party responsible for the disappearance of my address: Google.

Up until recently I had resisted the overbearing pull of digital life. Even now I wear with smug pride my badge of honor: my lack of a Facebook profile. I have, however, succumbed to LinkedIn, to posting lectures on YouTube, to reading online articles of the New York Times (of which I have a paid subscription). That is to say, despite my age, I have learned enough to become digitally literate.

I have also, on occasion, Googled myself. Up until recently my name elicited 125,000 results, several of which related to me and garnered the first page. The top results were as follows:

> Professor R—Full-time faculty—The C— College of Arts and Letters

> *20,000 Words Across the Sea—Translating Jules Verne*, EBSCHO host

> 'Ranking the English translations of Victor Hugo' with Professor R—, Youtube.com

And of course, the ubiquitous *www.ratemyprofessor.com* postings—such as:

> *Omg! Don't take his class. For real. I've had several professors wink at me, etc., but none were as blatantly repulsy as R—. He's a perv! Take my advice and switch 190 for 185 with Professor C—. Now that man is a dreamyahct ;)*

(Having no recollection of the student or the infamous 'wink…etc.,' I nevertheless was disheartened at the posting. But I was not deterred. I had begun to take a mild pleasure in proof of my place within the digital universe.)

While the Post Office took their time in investigating my missing address, I took it upon myself to find myself. There was a textbook for a seminar I planned to teach next semester that I had considered assigning for some time. I decided to purchase a used copy on Amazon.com. To make such a purchase on Amazon you must set up a personal account, linked to your email address and home address. After typing in the requisite information and pressing continue, I was surprised by a bold, red, outlined *Important Message:*

The street name or number appears to be invalid.

I doubled-checked the information and tried again. But my home address was unavoidably invalid. Which was impossible. I've lived at the same address for over a decade, and never before had I experienced any such problem. I fidgeted in indignation and Googled my address to prove to the Post Office and the internet and myself of its validity.

I entered my ZIP code. I clicked on Google Maps. I zoomed into my location. There was West Grove. There was the long slender finger of White Oaks Terrace, pointing to my street; pointing to the little dead end we called Forest Creek Road; pointing at nothing.

I stared in disbelief at the pixelated fuzz. Where was my beautiful street? Missing were the half-dozen houses, including mine, which lined its pavement. Yes, it's true that every house (except mine) on the block had been foreclosed; yes, every neighbor (except me) had been forced out; but even an abandoned street must appear to a satellite. Entire streets do not disappear overnight. It makes no difference to a satellite if the people are gone or not; it still must acknowledge the existence of Forest Creek Road. (In actuality, there wasn't 'nothing' where the street had been. The road and the houses had been replaced on the indiscriminate map by a camouflage clump of forest.)

> **I *stared in disbelief at the pixelated fuzz. Where was my beautiful street?***

Within the 'Help' section of Google Maps I filled out their standard form to report a problem. I requested to be updated by email when the problem was resolved. I replicate my personal inquiry as follows:

Dear Google,

I live just outside the city of G— in an unincorporated housing development called West Grove. More accurately, I live off White Oaks Terrance at 7858 Forest Creek Road. This address, however, is not found on any Google search. When using Google Maps, a supposedly reputable program with 'advanced satellite imaging,' I find the entire street of Forest Creek Road to have completely disappeared. Please fix the error as soon as you can. Please return Forest Creek Road to your Maps.

Thank you,
Professor R—

I received, within 48 hours:

Dear Professor R—,

It has been brought to our attention that the street you refer to, 'Forest Creek Road,' was recently deleted from Google Maps. This street was originally inserted into the map as a 'Trap Street' (a fictitious marking used by our cartographers to prevent copyright infringement) in an earlier version of Google Maps. It has since been deleted, due to the numerous complaints regarding the veracity of our maps and the confusion over a non-existent street. We apologize for the mistake. There will be no further communication from Google regarding this matter. I hope this helps. (Any subsequent inquiries into this matter will be viewed as a prank and ignored.)

Sincerely,

The Google team

A trap street. I had never heard of a trap street. A cursory investigation told me it was (as 'the Google team' had said) a mostly outdated practice by mapmakers to distinguish their work and discourage unauthorized reproduction. But this was impossible. There are 'trap streets' which are purposely false, and there are trap streets—like Forest Creek Road—which are real streets, horribly misidentified as a fabrication and wrongfully deleted.

I stood up from my desk and looked out the window. There was the street; the pothole two driveways down, the man-hole cover at the turn onto White Oaks, the half-dozen houses with their 'for-sale' signs; all there and accounted for (by me, at least).

My ensuing letters (tirades) to Google were ignored, as promised. I wasted whole days on the phone. I kept searching for the existence of my street online, with no result. Staring out the window for so long, I finally settled upon a method to prove the existence of my street. The foreclosed homes of my departed neighbors were owned by a local bank and managed by their real-estate department, as advertised in the phone number across the top of their for-sale signs. I called the number.

I learned the real-estate portfolio of the local bank had been bought by a larger, nationwide bank. I was given the number of the larger bank. After several minutes wait, I was connected to a real-estate representative with the larger bank.

"Hello, I'm interested in your properties on Forest Creek Road near G—."

"Of course, let me check…I'm sorry, I'm not finding anything. Which properties did you say?"

"There are half a dozen homes on Forest Creek Road. Near G—. Your bank recently acquired them, so maybe they aren't listed in your system yet."

"I'm still not finding anything, and our system is up-to-date."

"But that can't be."

"I'm sorry, sir, but there are no records of any such properties."

I stammered my objections for barely a minute before I was disconnected.

I spent a week, disconnected, purloined of my sense of place. At my lowest point I Googled myself (I sought any method for confirmation of my existence). But over the week the 'Problem' had spread. Google sought to finish me off. I was a discarded Petri dish, and the culture an unchecked Googlepox.

What had happened? My address had disappeared, yes. But now, not even a search of my own name revealed any of its past results. Instead, as my road had been replaced by a forest, now my identity had been replaced by another's.

I stared at the search results for this new, mutant Professor R—. Worms of blue font wriggled into letters sinister and unfamiliar, spelling my digital death. My grave from which they wriggled: the white, blank slate of the Google search page background.

How did I react when I found I was to be subjected to analog oblivion? I fidgeted and fussed. Where were my records? My works? The electronic proof of my existence? Had they completely disappeared? I clicked next, next, next—page 2 page 3 page 20. I burned through 125,000 plus results and found no mention of the man I knew as myself. What did I find? A viral stranger, who had emerged from the internet ether to steal my corporeality; who swapped his fate for mine, and turned me into a virtual ghost. Let us observe this new Professor R——. The top results were as follows:

Professor R——, Professor of the Joys of Exhibitionism

An Exhibitionist with a View, a blog with a lengthy series of graphic stories and photos (nudes, where every part above the shoulders is out of frame, and every part below the waist is well-lit)

Censored YouTube videos

Blurred Facebook photos (and unblurred)

You get the idea.

How I longed to put a face to this new 'me.' But there was only… This faceless, meddlesome member had replaced me on Google.

I am sure, but I'll never be certain, that somewhere in Mountain View, California, some lower-level Google staffers were infected by the bane of idleness. In a fit of my own impotent anger I imagine a conversation at the Googleplex headquarters. I see an elaborate break-room. I see two men—boys—on either side of a ping-pong table, lazily knocking back and forth a plastic ball, participating in an even lazier conversation.

"Did you finish the code for today?"

"Yeah, it was easy. Did you?"

"Yeah. I've been working on something else, though."

He misses the ball and serves again. "Oh, word? What is it?"

"Well, I made this program that randomly generates names and birthdays."

"What's the point?"

"I mean, I was just bored. But it's turned out pretty cool. I've found some real people. It's actually hilarious."

"You just find random people? That's it?"

"Well, yeah. Why?"

"We work at Google, dude! Let's fuck with them!"

"Ok, that could be good. We could spam their Gmail?"

"Yeah, if you're a fucking pussy. Or we could erase their existence from this world!"

"Haha! Let's do it!"

And my idle students. Always Googling. Always online, always chirping, searching, copying-pasting whole paragraphs into papers. I know where they developed their tired opinions on Flaubert. I know of their examples on literary naturalism in Zola. To them: J'accuse…! It came from Wikipedia. Their damned searches; their damned copying-pasting; their damned send send send, unrelenting to the end, until everyone can find them.

I curse their digital lives…

They came for me during my office hours. Not the students (they never come), but the Dean, the Departmental Chair, and an unarmed University Police Officer. They informed me I had thirty minutes to pack up my things before I was to be escorted off campus and never allowed to return. I spent twenty-five minutes explaining their mistake (a minute for every year spent on the job). I am not the person that it says I am on Google! That's not me! There's another, who's coopted my good name, whose blurred pictures have blotted out my good works!

With five minutes left he hurriedly packs his things, half-listening over his anger as they insist the evidence is heavily stacked against him. An emergency session was convened. There was lengthy testimony from students. *He insists he'll appeal. Vague ways to appeal are mentioned, but then the thirty minutes are up and the unarmed University Police Officer steps between him and his former colleagues and escorts him down the stairs and out the door. And to his car, where he's warned of the legal consequences if he returns.*

I arrived home earlier than usual. I called to order a pizza. As the phone rang, I contented myself with the image of a red delivery car, its plastic taxicab-like sign attached to the roof, turning off White Oaks Terrace and rolling down Forest Creek Road, solving every last one of my problems. I ordered the pizza, gave them my address, and felt relief when they told me it would be there in thirty minutes, guaranteed.

An hour passed before I called again. They said the attempt to deliver the pizza had failed. There was a mistake with the address. They said they could redeliver the pizza to a different address, but they would need to double check the address this time before they guaranteed its delivery. I told them not to bother.

A trap street can be a nasty surprise for any map-using journeyman, like a pizza-delivery boy. It's a nastier surprise to find out your own street is a trap street. It's the kind of surprise that can finally unhinge the last bolted door of sanity within your mind, and open it to all sorts of undisciplined chaos. What begins with the death of a postman ends with the aborted delivery of a pizza. You say, 'the road is real;' you keep saying, 'it's real to me.' Over and over. But no one else is there to console you. No one can find you.

There at the end of the paved street of your own damnation you sit. There you wait. There you rot, from the outside in, watching a road grow in your mind from a dark coil into the emptiness of the universe. You get up and go outside, afraid at first. You set foot on the road. It's not so bad, a little hot where the sun warmed it during the day, that's all. But those damn birds. Chirping idly above you. Surely they see the road. Look—bird shit. You scratch at white bird shit on the asphalt. You rub it between your fingers and stare at the birds and you know that they know about your road, they see it too, but you must be satisfied with a *chirp* if you want reassurance. Or maybe you're not satisfied. Maybe you get in your car and drive, return to civilization. Onto White Oaks Terrace. Google loves White Oaks Terrace. There you feel Google's love. The satellites look down on you. You are smiled upon. You want to always experience such love. But Google can't find you. No one can find you.

You stop at a park.

Hello, you say, would you like to get in my car? I would like to show you my road, you say. Please, get in my car; it's only a few minutes away. I just want to show you my road. It's funny, because nobody believes me, but it's there, over there, like this park. (You are told the police have been called).

You stop at a gas station.

Hello, you say, once you've filled up, why don't you follow me in your car to my road? Yes, safely in your car follow my car. I live off White Oaks Terrace. It's really close, over that way. Please, I'd just like to show you my road. But we must leave now because I think if I'm not there then my road might cease to exist. Won't you share its existence with me? (You are told the police have been called).

Before you leave, you fill up a gas can at the gas station.

Driving home, nighttime now, you turn off White Oaks Terrace onto Forest Creek Road. The lights are off in the half-dozen empty homes. A siren throbs in the distance but you know you are safe. They won't find you. The road protects you now. You are home. You are safe. No one can find you. The road protects you.

You pull into your driveway. You habitually stop at your mailbox. You discover mail for the first time in months (coupons, bills, etc.). Your problem has been addressed. You feel nauseous. You will be found. You walk inside and sit at your desk. You close your eyes and let the road swallow your mind.

You see the possibility to transmogrify the road. You redefine yourself as a chisel. You chip away at the road in your mind. Each fragment you chip away is a letter. You busy yourself, chipping away at the road, elated as each fragment, each letter, accumulates until you have a series of letters, thousands of letters which tumble through a faux-antique fountain pen in your hand onto a manuscript. You busy yourself filling the manuscript, reforming the road, transforming its dark coil into words on a page, freeing your mind. You raise your chisel a final time. The last chunk of road separates into two letters which fall on the page. Your mind is free. Your work is done. The burden of your road is now on the page. You rejoice in translating the terror of an object into the malleability of a manuscript. You walk to the end of your driveway. You do not see the road; the road is no longer where it was. Its chiseled remains are in the manila envelope you put in the mailbox. The bird shit appears to float in a void. *Search-copy-paste-send until everyone can find me.* You raise the flag on the mailbox. You return to your home. You keep busy. You write. You immolate your person. You continue to exist.

The 10-Million-Dollar Pillow

I NEVER READ PLATO'S Republic. I never considered a Master-Slave dialectic. I never even read *The Three Musketeers*.

I'll nod and agree with you when you say "the book is better than the movie." But where you spent the years of your youth washing dishes, serving tables, filling drinks, reading Cervantes, Shakespeare, and Fitzgerald, I didn't.

I've turned three-star Lonely Planet getaways into four-star destinations. I've topped charts, set box office records, and bedded bunnies, angels, and Kardashians.

I even have a 10-million-dollar pillow. It was a gift from me to me, on my 26th birthday. Because what do you get the man who has slept with everything?

What do you get the man who has slept with everything?

My head has enjoyed that pillow about twenty times. It's at the house I'm about to sell.

So, why does it cost $10 XL Ms?

Perhaps it's the cotton spun by octogenarian Utter Pradesh millswomen, blind since birth, who hand-spin using techniques passed down fifteen generations.

Perhaps it's the baby-chick feathers of the German Water Fowl, that in the summers migrate to the Ugandan side of Lake Victoria, where it feasts on freshwater crill, allowing it to grow the softest and most durable feathers on the planet.

Perhaps it's the vacuum seal, when packaging the pillow case in low earth orbit, that crisps and removes any dust, giving the pillow the natural smell of metallic nothingness.

Perhaps it's the decade before the first night of the pillow, the ten years of my work plus thousands of hours of self-doubt and externally originated hate, that make me ponder the purchase at 11:33 pm on a Tuesday night.

Maybe it's the fact that every pillow I've ever owned has cost less than 100 dollars, and has never given me a second thought.

Whoever spent more than five minutes deciding on a pillow? And yet, as my finger hesitates before I click on the last photo of the website, as I consider the pillow with the thousand-year pedigree, sewn with threads picked from the shroud of Turin, jabbed with a needle made from narwhal horn and rubbed with the indistinguishable scent of a newborn panda, I have a second thought that lasts an eternity.

Your years made my 10-million-dollar pillow. Your youth makes my head comfortable. And when I sleep, I dream of Marcus Aurelius's *Meditations*.

I'm in a small inner tent on the Roman front in Sirimium, at a desk with a quill in my hand, the winds of the plain heard rippling the tent's shell, on the eve of battle, and I'm drafting a sentence with just the right amount of wordplay and forthrightness. It takes me hours to come up with the right order of words. And when I finally decide on the exact arrangement of expression, and the several words that will do the trick, I feel exalted, as if I've experienced a final victory in battle. Unlike your dreams, this exhalative moment endures, the feeling of triumph prevails, and it seems I live a lifetime in that moment. And just as the feeling wanes, the vividness of the moment becomes perverse, and I see its colors as grotesque. A feeling of unnatural orientation obscures my thoughts. It's then that I awake on the 10-million-dollar pillow.

I awake as Marcus Aurelius, a Roman Emperor, actualized. The 10 million dollars have transformed my sense of self.

And when you wake, and raise your head from your pillow, you dream of nothing.

The Gondolier

FOG, HEAVY ON the *Laguna Veneta*, obscured the bell tower of *San Giorgio Maggiore* on the right and the banks of the *Lido* in the distance. Nothing but the weighted bow, combing through the mist, was visible to the tireless rower.

He stood at the stern of the gondola, as he had for years, sometimes verbose and sometimes silent, but always his eyes forward, vigilantly watching for each bend in the canal, for each destined mooring. There were times when the muscles of his shoulders ached, when his knees shook and his hands grew weary about the oar; but his eyes never tired. For even then, as he stared through the layers of fog rolling in from the Adriatic toward the mainland, he looked for her.

* * *

He had first seen her clothed in white, in the Abyssinian manner, her tanned hands clutching the front of her dress to lift her hem, her exposed feet stepping into the uncut emerald waters of Lake Tana. She was among a large crowd of locals gathered about the banks that day. Her reserved smile became playful as she waded into the water, up to her hips, among a group of other women similarly covered in white.

"Why do they bathe with their clothes on?" he had asked Captain Bonbiolo as they cut through a grove of fig trees shading the banks where the crowd had gathered.

"They aren't bathing, young Benetto. They are worshipping. It is Timkat, the festival of the Epiphany."

Benetto approached the gathering with Captain Bonbiolo and the few other conquering Italian officers stationed at the *Residenza* in Gorgora, Amhara Province, Ethiopia. A group of local priests, costumed in hues as varied as birds-of-paradise, passed the Italians in khaki.

"The priests have blessed the water," Captain Bonbiolo said, nodding at the retreating procession. "Care for a swim?"

Benetto assented absently. He watched her laugh as a group of boys splashed in the water. The other women were leaving but she walked out slowly. Benetto removed his boots alongside Captain Bonbiolo and the other officers. When she walked onto the sandy beach, he paused to watch her dainty toes surface from the water. He tried to recall the small face that looked at his, but after so many decades it was becoming impossible. He recalled the sensation in his gut, however, and the color of her cheeks as she looked away; flushed, a tinge of pink, like a blooming tamarisk.

The gondolier sustained the vision in his mind, even as a blackness began to creep in and dim the joy of the memory. A blackness dark and shiny; like motor oil, or the crisp black uniform of *Centurione* Mancini, the leader of the volunteer *Milizia* garrison also stationed in Gorgora. The *Milizia* blackshirts, compared to the regular troops stationed at the *Residenza,* were hardliner Fascists; and none more so than Mancini, their commanding officer. With a thin frame and an awkward stride, the only thing mildly formidable about *Centurione* Mancini was the groomed mustache on his upper lip, as sharp as a *stiletto*, and the threat of the party he represented. *Centurione* Mancini arrived at the lake separately that day, and hailed the attention of Captain Bonbiolo's party. Captain Bonbiolo gestured a half-hearted salute as Mancini approached.

"You'd never guess these pagan blacks were Christian," the *Centurione* said after a stiff salute.

"No," replied Captain Bonbiolo, sweating into his khakis, as the distant grunt of a hippopotamus floated over the calm lake. "On that account you are correct."

Centurione Mancini looked disapprovingly at the bare feet of Bonbiolo's men sinking into the wet sand.

"You weren't planning on joining this frivolous spectacle, were you Captain?"

The stout chest of Captain Bonbiolo deflated almost imperceptibly. "No, *Centurione*. Only cooling off our toes, to relieve the heat of the day. But, it is fortunate you happened on us here, for there is a subject I've desired to bring up with you. If you'd like to accompany me on a light walk so that we might talk privately—"

"Anything you have to say can be said here without delay." The *stiletto* twitched as the eyes above it observed Benetto gazing at the native women. "I, as well, have something I must bring up with you. So what is it?"

"I and my men have come up with the idea of having a Canoe Club here in Gorgora, for the purposes of fitness and morale. We would like to extend an invitation toward the men of the *Milizia*, if they'd like to participate."

"My men are occupied with separate matters. But I must insist that your club include no native members. We are occupiers, Captain, and there must be no fraternization with those we occupy. Which brings me to my point."

"Yes?"

"You are aware of Il Duce's edict concerning the commingling and cohabitation of Italians with the feminine filth of this country? The purity of our blood is at stake. I've seen the horde of women sneaking from your barracks every dawn. You must control your men, or someone will do the job for you."

Captain Bonbiolo admirably contained a smirk. "I will see to it personally, my *Centurione*."

The two men exchanged salutes and separated. As soon as Mancini was out of earshot the officers began to protest the new edict of Mussolini's, which forbade their greatest escape from the daily African inferno—the soft company of native women in the cool evenings.

"Enough," said Captain Bonbiolo. "You heard the *Centurione*. We must substitute one sport for another." He looked longingly at the cluster of wet figures in white dancing in the lake. "Let us hope the canoeing can provide us with exhilaration enough to ease our other humors."

The men turned from the shore muttering quiet obscenities at the distant back of *Centurione* Mancini. Benetto was the last to leave. He stared at the girl. She was seated on a large dry stone, looking across the lake at the vague form of Dek Island floating over the horizon, and at the distant shore beyond, imperceptible from such a low height, even on a clear day.

* * *

"Are we nearly there?" asked the passenger seated in the open cabin of the gondola as it bounced over the choppy waters of the *Laguna Veneta*.

"Are we nearly there?" asked the passenger seated in the open cabin of the gondola as it bounced over the choppy waters of the *Laguna Veneta.*

The somber gondolier lowered his gaze from the fog. The forgotten passenger—a tourist, his accent indefinable—shivered beneath lightweight travel clothes.

"No," replied the gondolier, his attention ever forward.

The tourist sighed, shifting his weight on a frayed cushion. "I appreciate you taking me out in this weather, as all the others turned me down. However, this voyage is beginning to seem quite interminable."

"I can tell you a story, if you like."

"That would be most welcome."

"There was the shore…" spoke the gondolier.

The boat swayed as the tourist lurched forward for a better look. "Where away? I thought you said we weren't there?"

"No," said the gondolier. "That is how my story begins. Content yourself to listen."

* * *

There was the shore, less than a hundred yards away, and young Benetto accelerated to get there first. He was standing in the stern of a tankwa, an indigenous boat made of bound papyrus reeds. When Benetto had first seen the tankwas crisscrossing Lake Tana, he suspected in them a primitive kinship with the evolved sophistication of the gondola. Tankwas were paddled solo from the stern, sometimes sitting and sometimes standing. Benetto immediately noticed their charm.

His addition to the tankwa, as a founding member of the Gorgora Canoe Club, was the *forcola*. The defining feature of any Venetian gondola, the *forcola*, basically a curved oarlock, was a mechanism attached at the stern through which was inserted the oar. This allowed the gondolier the ease, speed, and dexterity that was unique to his craft. With a crude *forcola* attached to the tankwa, Benetto was able to row the native boat in a fashion near enough to the gondolas of Venice.

Earlier that day, during his allotted free time, Benetto had gone out on his own to test his *forcola*-equipped tankwa. He maintained his balance without incident, but had difficulty maneuvering the tankwa with the same sharp angles as was required to spin from one canal to the next back home in Venice. While rowing his boat around in circles, Benetto casually noticed the approach of a native paddler, who propelled his tankwa while seated. Benetto hailed him with a whistle, and the native paused his paddling. Benetto used his oar to mime a brisk rowing, and after several attempts at confused gestures the native understood the Italian's desire to race.

The native's tankwa accelerated faster than Benetto's, but after a series of firm and even strokes Benetto matched his rival's speed. He noticed the native used an oar with two paddles, propelling himself with alternating strokes from left to right. It required much more effort than the rhythmic cranking of his oar in the *forcola*.

And there was the shore, less than a hundred yards away. Benetto soon passed the native, who began to tire from the exertion of the sprint. Moments before Benetto's tankwa glided onto the sandy bottom of the shoreline, he noticed up the bank the same young girl he had seen at the festival of Timkat, seated on the same stone at the edge of the lake, watching him. He nearly lost his balance.

The native paddler leaned forward in his tankwa to steady a load of wood threatening to cascade overboard as the boat ground ashore. Benetto heard unintelligible mutterings which seemed to show little regard for sportsmanship.

"I'm sorry, friend. I speak some of the native tongue, but I can't understand a word you're saying. It does seem as if you're not handling defeat too well."

The young girl descended from her stone. "*Signore*," she said.

Benetto was startled to hear her speak. Though Italian was a language ignorant to the people of Gorgora, they did at least address Italians as such.

She continued in conventional Amhara, the language of the province, of which Benetto knew enough to understand her. "You do not understand him because he speaks a tribal dialect. I will speak his words so you understand. He says: 'his boat was weighted with firewood. He wonders if the *signore* could manage to win if his boat had been empty.'"

"Unburden your boat, and let's go again."

The native paddler began to remove the logs from his tankwa. Benetto reached for his oar and was about to push his boat from the shore when the girl spoke.

"Wait," she said. "He unburdens his boat, but not to race again."

"Why?"

"It is forbidden. A *signore* and a native cannot row together." The girl translated as the paddler spoke again. "'He desires only to bring the wood to his family. He does not want any trouble."

"Trouble? It is late, there are no *Milizia* watching."

"No, *signore*. His tribe respects the ancient ways of these waters. He believes lost souls wander the lake at night. He does not want to trouble them."

Benetto looked at the face of the native girl. Her brown eyes reflected the waters of Lake Tana behind him. She remained silent as the paddler retired with his bundle and left them alone.

"I remember you from Timkat," Benetto said. "You are the girl who loves the water."

"I also remember you," she replied. "You are the boy who stares at me. You are very skilled with the tankwa."

Benetto was about to reply when a forlorn wail floated over the lake. The two shifted their gaze to the waters.

"Is it one of those lost spirits?" asked Benetto.

"Perhaps."

Benetto climbed atop the stone and stared at the lake. "Is this why you stare at the water?" he asked her. "Are you waiting for a lost soul?"

"No," she replied. "No one seeks to find me."

"But how can that be, when I have been seeking you, in my dreams."

The pink flush returned to her face. "Good evening, *signore*," she said, turning in a hurry.

"Wait," he called after her. She stopped. "Ancient Italians had a similar belief as your tribesman," he said as she turned around. "They believed the spirit, after death, had to cross a river by ferry before entering the afterlife. Those who did not cross wandered the underworld, lost."

"Your people believed our souls are lost if they cannot cross the water?"

"Yes," Benetto said as he looked across the lake. "And now I see what you desire. You sit here and stare at the horizon. You desire to cross these waters and leave this place."

"Yes," she replied. "I desire to escape."

"There are many ways to escape."

"But you contemplate one."

"Yes. I know of a way we may escape together."

"Yes. I know of a way we may escape together."

A smile straightened the sad curvature of her eyes and Benetto stepped off the stone, towards her. She backed up, careful to preserve the distance between them in public.

"You must visit me tonight," he said.

"Perhaps," she replied. "I will come to the barracks as the other women do. You will be my *signore*."

"Benetto," he said. "That is my name."

"I am Gelila," she replied, "and tonight you will not have to dream of me."

* * *

The tourist straightened up and grinned at the gondolier. "This story is starting to get good."

The gondolier rowed without interruption.

* * *

She arrived with the other women late that night. The two escaped beneath the sweaty cotton sheets of his bed. They learned the wondrous surfaces and infinite depths of their bodies. At the hour when the other women left, Benetto asked her to stay. It was nearly dawn when, resting in the comfort of his arms, she finally looked away from him and whispered, "I must go." He nodded, and watched her brown skin disappear into the white of her dress, and the whiteness fade into a dull grey as she passed into the faint light of the early morning. He closed his eyes, and was attempting to recall the rhythm of her breathing when roll call was sounded, an hour earlier than usual. This was done occasionally as an emergency drill, but no drill was scheduled for today.

He dressed and ran from the barracks, ill at ease, falling in line with the other men. Every man assembled was similarly confused by the nature of the drill. When Captain Bonbiolo approached the head of the assembly, with *Centurione* Mancini marching beside, Benetto understood with horror what was about to occur.

"Men," began Captain Bonbiolo, his voice pained, as Mancini watched in delight. "There has been a direct violation of orders from Rome. One of you has been caught cohabitating with a native woman."

The assembled soldiers chuckled, failing to notice the zeal exposed in the eyes of Mancini.

"Silence!" shouted *Centurione* Mancini. "There will be an example made."

Benetto's eyes lost focus as a brown woman in white was marched forward.

Mancini grabbed Gelila by a clump of curls in her hair. "Who among you defiled himself with this whore?" Gelila whimpered in pain as Mancini twisted his grip.

It was too much for Benetto.

"It was I, *Centurione* Mancini. I was with her."

Mancini pushed Gelila's head away and turned to Captain Bonbiolo. "There you have it, Captain. Now deal with your men."

Captain Bonbiolo turned his sad eyes toward Benetto for a brief moment, offering a silent apology, before he looked away.

Benetto was sentenced to a month of isolation in the stockade. He was not told what happened to Gelila. He spent the month thinking only of her; of her body immersed in the waters of Lake Tana; of his body immersed within hers.

* * *

"Poor kids," said the tourist. "They didn't deserve it."

* * *

When Benetto was released, he discovered he no longer held the same rank as before. He also discovered his membership in the Canoe Club had been revoked. The nights within the barracks were now quiet. No women arrived; the shame was too great for the exposed woman; the punishment too serious for the exposed man. After a week spent outside the stockade, but trapped inside the walls of the *Residenza* without word of Gelila, Benetto's thoughts turned desperate.

One afternoon, when Benetto was feeling especially low, Captain Bonbiolo approached him for the first time since he had been punished.

"Don't bother saluting, Benetto, I don't deserve it. I've been feeling like such an ass about what happened."

"It's not your fault, Captain, everybody knows that. You were only following orders."

"Following orders—an excuse that sends a man to hell. You don't have to say anything Benetto. I only came here to tell you that at the Club's *regatta* the other day, where you were sorely missed by everyone, I happened upon your young lady sitting beside the lake, watching the men and the boats. She was desperate to see you. I'm telling you this now because the *Centurione* is away on party business in Gondar tonight, and you should expect a visitor."

Benetto looked at his Captain in surprise.

"It's the least I can do, young Benetto." Captain Bonbiolo nodded before he politely excused himself.

Later that night, Gelila returned to Benetto's bed. They melted at each other's touch; immersed, they calmly waded beyond shallow waters, further than ever before, until each drowned in the other.

"We must escape," she said, breathless, as dawn finally approached.

"Again?"

"No. We must leave this place. Together." The rhythm of her heart accelerated.

"We will leave tomorrow," Benetto said. "I will meet you at dawn at the place where we first met, with my tankwa, and together we will escape by rowing from Gorgora across Lake Tana—as far as Bahir Dar if we have to."

"I will be there."

She left him then, and when Benetto heard no alarm and roll was called at the usual hour he knew there was hope for their success. The day passed without incident. Well after midnight, after every human sound in the area had long since faded and as the moon began to set, Benetto stole from the barracks and exited the *Residenza* for the final time. He crept toward the shore of the nearby lake, where the Canoe Club managed a small dock where the different boats were moored. Here Benetto found his modified tankwa, lulling idly in wait for its creator.

The village of Gorgora was along the coast, half a league to the south from the *Residenza*. Benetto pushed off from the dock and gently cranked the oar in the *forcola*, the one human sound in the night amongst an infinite chorus of nature. The night was cool, the waters still beneath ghostly wisps of fog that began to drift from the lake and settle over the village in the distance.

After half an hour, Benetto was immersed in the fog, his eyes strained forward, expecting the shore any moment. There was nothing but the water and the fog. He began to worry, began to think he had lost his way in the weather, that the sun would rise and the fog would disappear and he would be alone, and in his absence she would believe their love offered no escape. His eyes begged the shore to appear, for the fog to vanish, for her to be standing there on her stone waiting for him.

The ghost of a forlorn voice drifted over the water.

"Gelila!" he roared.

* * *

"Look—a figure!" shouted the tourist, standing up and nearly pitching from the gondola in surprise.

The gondolier looked up through the visions of his memory into the receding fog. A lone figure appeared on the looming shore.

"We have arrived," said the gondolier, his voice grim.

The tourist blinked as the fog thinned to nothing, replaced by a foreign shore that looked volcanic, a jagged sharpness shining black. "I thought the sun would be up already," said the tourist. "Haven't you brought me to the *Lido*?"

The gondolier kept his eyes on the approach to the shore. "Where we are, the sun neither rises nor sets."

"You did agree to bring me to the other side," insisted the tourist. "You were the only one, in that damned fog. It is your duty as a gondolier to fulfill your obligation."

"I have done my duty. I have brought you to the other side."

The waves around the gondola, breaking on the shallows, splashed the tourist. He instantly felt a chill, felt it prickle his entire body, cooling every part of him, until it got to his heart, which was still.

"Where are we?" he asked, looking from the black shore toward the stern face of the gondolier.

The gondolier spoke. "We are in the underworld, on the River Styx, and I have brought you to your destination."

"I'm dead?" the tourist asked, his hand searching the void within his chest.

"Yes," said the gondolier.

"And you are the ferryman?"

* * *

Young Benetto noticed the shallowness of the water as the fog began to part and knew he had arrived. He saw the vague outline of the shore. And there was a figure there, alone, dressed in white. He hurried his strokes, desperate to be away with her before the sun rose. His tankwa was about to skid onto the sand when a blackness materialized behind the white. Too late, he saw the figure waiting for him was *Centurione* Mancini, holding a drawn pistol, eyes reflecting the cloudy greyness of the fog. Benetto gave his oar a frantic twist, as he had managed a thousand times in the canals of Venice. But the modified tankwa was not built for such a move. The boat rolled, and Benetto tumbled head first into the water. He longed to break his neck, or drown, but when *Centurione* Mancini pulled his head from the water he knew his fate was worse.

* * *

"Before I was killed, I was told she was still alive. Somehow, someway, she had survived whatever was inflicted upon her. I do not know why she yet lived, or what she had been forced to do. I did not care what the others said. To me, all that mattered was for us to be together again. I was unable to search for her in that life, however. I was shot the next day for desertion. And so I died. But I could not rest in peace. Not without her. And now I wait."

The gondola glided onto a narrow beach of volcanic sand. The tourist had no immediate urge to exit, especially as the unknown figure on the black shore materialized into view. The unknown figure, an old man with a white beard and a kind face, wore a ragged tunic, and limped forward on a wooden leg.

"Charon," said the gondolier, hailing the bearded old man. "I've got another one here for you."

"Hello, Benetto," the old man addressed the gondolier. His voice was gentle and warm, and did much to dispel the tourist's alarm. "Is this the one?"

"No," said the gondolier, nodding at the tourist. "This one is yours."

"Very well." Charon extended his hand toward the boat and the tourist reached for it, without fear. He felt as if the old man were a distant family member, or a forgotten friend. The old man pointed at a worn path that wound inland, through the volcanic blackness. The tourist walked up the banks, his being more at peace with each step, while the old man remained behind.

Benetto stirred the waters of the River Styx, turning the boat around.

The old man looked on, and when he spoke his voice was tender. "Dear Benetto, when will you be done? You cannot do my job forever."

As the turned the boat around, Benetto's eyes remained set ever forward. "You are right, Charon. But I will continue your job, ferrying the dead, for as long as it takes. Until her body fades and her spirit is freed. Until that moment when the fog parts, and I see my love standing on the shores of the underworld.

In that moment she will be there waiting for me, and I will be there to take her away on my boat. And we will rescue each other from our lost lives. Nothing else will matter—not death or life or the shifting tides of the universe. For we will be together on the voyage to cross these waters, and together we will reach our final shore. Only then, dear Charon, will I consent to give you back your boat."

The Delivery

"**I**T'S JUST NOT what I was expecting," said Samantha. She held up the delivery in her outstretched hands. *What the hell?* she wondered.

She had ordered it forever ago. Wanting the one in blush pink, she was certain she had double-checked her choice of color before checkout. But this one was more lavender than blush.

"Let's send it back. Get a refund," said her husband, Mark, sitting in a chair beside Samantha. He squirmed, suppressing frustration. He was half-pissed at the delivery error, half-pissed at Samantha, whom he suspected of *not* double-checking the choice of color before checkout. And the delivery fucker had just left, so the two of them were stewing alone with *it* in the room now.

"For real," she said, turning it over. "It's smaller, too."

Samantha was doing her best to keep her cool. Sure, mistakes happen—but not like this. Not to her, on such an important order, which had taken months to arrive. *In all that time, did nobody check to make sure they got the order right?* She wanted to know who was responsible.

"Oh god," said Mark, looking at his phone. "It's like two pounds lighter than advertised. Something's missing."

Did Samantha not order from the link I sent her? Mark wondered. He was seriously questioning whether or not she had even clicked on the correct link.

Samantha set it down. She was near her breaking point. "I think somebody's fucking with us. Like this is a joke to them."

Mark nodded. When you place an order, you do so with the expectation that what you order is what you'll get. You put your trust in others, whom you pay to deliver the order as advertised. This is not what happened today. It did seem like a terrible joke. *Or had Samantha messed up and she was avoiding admitting to her mistake?* Either way, Mark was ready to explode.

"Let's talk to him," he said. "That delivery fucker."

"Yeah" she said. "He's probably still outside. Go bring him back here."

Mark went out the door and shouted for the delivery fucker. While waiting, Samantha closed her eyes, barely able to contain her irritation. She took a deep breath. Calm for a moment, she had the space for a second thought: *Maybe lavender will be okay?*

Then she opened her eyes and looked back at it. "Oh my god," she said, aggravated more than before. "It's like completely violet now." Her voice caught in her throat. "What the hell—did they send one that *changes colors?*"

"Jesus fucking Christ," said Mark. He was almost positive now that Samantha had fucked up the order. But he wasn't going to explode at her. Not now. Not before he had it out with the delivery fucker.

There was a knock, then the delivery fucker stepped inside.

"This is unacceptable," said Samantha before Mark could get in the first word. She held it up. "We didn't order violet."

It did indeed look violet. Even an off-putting, sickly violet.

It did indeed look violet. Even an off-putting, sickly violet.

"We ordered blush pink," said Mark. "*Blush pink,*" he repeated for emphasis. "How are you going to make this right?"

The delivery fucker was apologetic. Samantha rolled her eyes. She wanted to scream—but at someone who was being defensive, not at someone who was saying "You're right" and "I'm sorry" in ten different ways.

"We don't need your scripted customer service apology," said Mark. "Just fix this."

The delivery fucker explained how there was a feature that would change settings from blush pink to lavender to violet, and back again. He fiddled with it, and within a minute it had changed back to its original setting: blush pink.

Samantha's eyes went wide. "It looks just like the picture!" she said, relief in her voice.

The delivery fucker handed it back to Samantha. Mark remained upset, mostly at the missed opportunity to explode. "It's still two pounds lighter than advertised."

Wouldn't this delivery fucker have an answer for everything, Mark thought sarcastically, as the delivery fucker explained how with proper care it should maintain the advertised weight.

Mark sat down with nothing further to say. Samantha, meanwhile, was smiling. Glowing, even. She thanked the delivery fucker, who left the room with a final apology and a "Congratulations!"

"Blush pink!" she exclaimed happily, holding it now in her arms. "And we just have to care for it right so the weight won't be an issue."

"Sure," said Mark, standing up. "And at least it's got all its fingers and toes. But why do they even have a violet setting, when all we really want is blush pink?"

About the Author

Eland Mann is a writer, editor, and entrepreneur.

A graduate of the George Washington University, he has worked as a magazine editor, freelance ghostwriter, and content writer, and was published on Yahoo.com and in *National Geographic Traveler Mongolia*, among others. After serving as a foreign correspondent in Mongolia for the news agency AFP, he worked as a managing editor and ghostwriter in hybrid publishing. In 2019 he co-founded hybrid publisher *Conversation Publishing*. He's helped hundreds of authors to create and publish a book.

He currently lives in Arlington, Virginia, with his wife, Khaliun, and two children, Marlowe and Lincoln. www.ElandMann.com